# THE GRAND STREET THEATER ROBBERY

Illustrations by Warwick Bennett

**Harcourt Achieve**

Rigby • Saxon • Steck-Vaughn

www.HarcourtAchieve.com
1.800.531.5015

**Rigby PM Extensions Chapter Books**
part of the Rigby PM Program
Emerald Level

Published by Harcourt Achieve Inc.
P.O. Box 27010, Austin, Texas 78755.

U.S. edition © 2005 Harcourt Achieve Inc.

First published in 2003 by Thomson Learning Australia
The Grand Street Theater Robbery Text © Thomson Learning
Australia 2003
Illustrations © Thomson Learning Australia 2003

10 9 8 7 6 5 4 3 2 1
07 06 05 04

Printed in China by 1010 Printing Limited

**The Grand Street Theater Robbery**
ISBN 0 7578 9361 9

# Contents

# CHAPTER 1

# STRANGE BEHAVIOR

"Did you hear that?" whispered Jed.

"What?" asked Rosie.

"Listen," said Jed, pointing at the wall of the adjoining apartment. He crept over and listened intently. Silence!

Why was it, wondered Jed, that he seemed to be the only one to hear Larry's strange behavior?

Larry had moved in next door a few months ago. He knew hundreds of great jokes, and he was very friendly, thought Jed. It was just that Larry acted so . . . weird.

He came and went at odd hours of the day and night, and sometimes he wore really strange clothes and spoke in weird accents.

When he first moved in, Larry told Dad he was a janitor. That might explain the strange hours he kept, but Jed had never heard of a janitor wearing fancy clothes to work!

And that wasn't the weirdest part.

Larry always seemed to be talking to someone in his apartment – loudly! Yet, as far as Jed could tell, Larry lived alone.

Something very odd seemed to be going on next door.

"Listen! There he goes again," said Jed.

This time Rosie listened with her ear against the wall. She grinned at Jed and started giggling. "You're right. He *is* talking to himself."

Jed held his finger over his lips. "Ssh! I can't hear what he's saying." A muffled voice came through the wall.

"Stand and deliver, sir. Hand over all your money and valuables."

Jed and Rosie looked at one another with wide eyes.

"Maybe that's why he acts so strange," said Jed. "He's really a robber."

"Don't be silly," said Rosie. "He's a janitor."

This time the voice boomed through the wall. "This is not a game. Give me all your money – now!"

Startled, Jed and Rosie jumped.

"See, I told you," said Jed, looking pleased with himself. "He must be a robber."

"Why would he be robbing someone in his own apartment?" asked Rosie.

"No, silly," said Jed. "He's practicing now for when he does a *real* robbery."

"Put your hands in the air. This is a hold up!" thundered the voice through the wall.

Jed and Rosie looked at one another.

Jed whispered, "Sounds like he's getting ready for a big bank robbery or something. What do you think we should do?"

That night, Jed lay awake staring at the ceiling, and thinking about Larry and what he might be planning to do. Should he tell Mom and Dad? What if he and Rosie were just imagining things?

His bedroom shared a wall with Larry's apartment, and he could tell that Larry wasn't home. It was very late when he heard Larry's front door slam.

Jed listened hard. Then he heard the sound of coins dropping onto the floor.

Had Larry been out robbing people tonight?

# CHAPTER 2

# THE ELEVATOR HOLD-UP

The next morning, Jed and Rosie stood outside the elevator in their apartment building. "We can't spy on him," said Rosie.

"Why not?" asked Jed. "I think he's planning a big robbery."

"But Dad said he's a janitor," argued Rosie. "And we've both seen him working at the theater."

Jed knew that Rosie was right.

Every afternoon on their way home from school they passed the Grand Street Theater. They often saw Larry sweeping the floors and polishing the windows.

"That could be a front," said Jed. "He could just be pretending to be a janitor, so no one will be suspicious."

The elevator beeped and the doors slid apart. Both the children's mouths dropped open.

There was Larry, glaring at his reflection in the mirrored walls. With a fierce frown, he yelled, "Put all the money in the bag – now!"

Jed and Rosie stood frozen in their spot.

Then he turned and saw the children. "Sorry if I startled you both. I want to sound convincing. Don't want anyone thinking I'm an amateur, do we?"

Jed and Rosie backed away, shaking their heads.

"Going down?" asked Larry.

"No thanks. We'll take the stairs," said Jed. And the pair fled down the hall.

# CHAPTER 3

# THE DISGUISE

The next day after school, Jed and Rosie went shopping with Mom.

"Look! It's him," hissed Jed. He nudged Rosie, and they both looked across the store to see Larry gazing intently at a counter filled with expensive watches.

They watched Larry move around the counter.

"Let's follow him," said Jed.

"I don't think we should," said Rosie. "Mom will be going soon."

Jed looked across at Mom. "She's busy talking to Mrs. Dean. She'll be quite a while yet."

They asked Mom if they could take a look around and meet her again in ten minutes. She nodded.

"Come on," whispered Jed to Rosie. "Let's find out what he's up to."

The pair followed Larry around the store. They hid behind displays and peeked out to see what Larry was doing.

Jed nudged Rosie. "Look over there."

Larry was in the next department, trying on a bushy black wig and a false beard.

"It's a disguise," hissed Jed.

"It probably doesn't mean anything," said Rosie. "Maybe he's got a costume party to go to."

"I'm sure it's a disguise," insisted Jed. "The big robbery must be soon."

For the next two afternoons Jed didn't watch television or play basketball. He sat on the landing outside his apartment building and pretended to be doing his homework. But really he was noting down when Larry came in and when he went out.

The hours ticked by slowly, and still Jed had no clue as to where or when the robbery would take place.

On the third day Jed stayed inside. He heard the phone ring in Larry's empty apartment. Then the elevator bell beeped and the doors swung open.

Jed peeked out in the hall. Larry stepped out of the elevator. He fumbled with his key in the lock, flung open the door of his apartment, and ran to pick up the phone.

Jed could hear him talking. He knew he should move away and not listen, but what if Larry was planning the robbery? This could be his big chance to find out.

He crept closer to Larry's door, listening hard. He heard him say nervously, "Tonight? Yes, yes, I'm ready."

There was a pause, then Larry spoke again. "I'll make sure there are no mistakes. The Grand Street Theater will be my biggest job yet. I'll be there at seven."

Oh, no, thought Jed. The robbery is tonight!

He crept back down the hall, and looked at his watch. It was 6:05 already! If he was going to stop Larry, he had to move fast.

# CHAPTER 4

# THE WARNING

Jed knew that there was a big show opening that night at the Grand Street Theater. The show would be packed and the ticket office would take in lots of money – and then Larry would come along and steal it!

Jed didn't want Larry to get into trouble, but he knew he had to do something to stop him.

Just then, Larry came running out of his apartment. He winked at Jed. "This is my big night. I can't afford to make a mistake. If I pull it off, everyone will be after me. Maybe you'll see my name on the posters."

"Wait!" yelled Jed.

But Larry wasn't stopping. "No time to chat."

Now Jed had no choice – it was time for drastic action!

As Larry charged past, Jed stuck out his foot. Larry tripped, but quickly regained his balance.

"Careful," he called to Jed. "I don't *really* want to break a leg."

Larry looked nervous and excited. In too much of a hurry to wait for the elevator, he dashed straight down the stairs.

Jed bit his lip. He was running out of ideas.

He hurried inside his apartment. He couldn't keep Larry's secret any longer. He had to tell Mom and Dad the whole story, but Dad was busy reading his newspaper and hardly listened. He just said, "I don't think you need to worry about Larry, but you will have to put a stopper in that imagination. One day it might get you into trouble."

Jed tried to tell Mom, but she said she was too busy getting dinner to play games.

Rosie shook her head and asked, "Are you still going on about that?"

Why won't anyone believe me? thought Jed. Everyone liked Larry, yet no one seemed to want to help stop him from making a big mistake.

Jed knew it was up to him.

When no one was looking, he picked up the telephone. He didn't want to get Larry into trouble, but maybe he could warn the police about a robbery at the theater. Then when Larry saw police everywhere, he wouldn't go through with his plan.

Jed was about to dial when Mom yelled, "Put that phone down at once and come to dinner. We'll be late."

"But, Mom . . . ," said Jed.

"Now!" insisted Mom.

"Where are we going?" asked Jed.

"We have tickets to a new show," Mom said.

Jed groaned. This would ruin his plans – he had a robbery to prevent.

He checked his watch. It was exactly seven o'clock.

Oh, no! It was too late to stop Larry now.

# CHAPTER 5

# THE SHOW MUST GO ON

Mom, Dad, Rosie, and Jed walked around the corner onto Grand Street.

Jed looked up at the bright lights all around the theater. He half expected to hear police sirens. But all was quiet apart from the excited voices of the theater-goers, and the rumble of passing cars.

Just then, they walked past the alley alongside the theater. Jed couldn't believe his eyes. There was Larry about to sneak in through the stage door.

"Don't do it, Larry," yelled Jed.

"Ssh! Jed," said Dad, with a frown.

"But Dad . . . ," pleaded Jed, starting off toward the stage door after Larry's retreating figure.

Dad tugged Jed's arm. "Come on, son, the show is about to start," he said.

Dad led them into the theater, and stopped to buy a program and some popcorn. When they found their seats, Jed fidgeted nervously. Was Larry at the ticket office right now, stuffing the takings into his bag?

The house lights dimmed and the music started. Several actors walked onto the stage, but Jed couldn't watch. He could only think about Larry.

Then he heard a familiar voice.

"Stand and deliver, sir. Hand over all your money and valuables!"

There on the stage, wearing a black wig and a false beard, Larry stood proudly acting out his robbery.

Rosie elbowed Jed in the ribs and said. "Ha! And you thought Larry was a robber."

Jed shuffled down in his seat. Suddenly it all made sense. His cheeks grew hot and red. He was glad the house lights were dark.

He didn't know how he'd managed to get everything so wrong. But it certainly had sounded like Larry was practicing a robbery.

Why didn't he guess Larry was only acting?

Jed knew he'd have to apologize to Larry tomorrow. Perhaps he could make up for spying on him by helping him learn his lines.

And silently he made a promise.

Next time he heard Larry rehearse, he'd ask him what type of part he was playing ... before he let his imagination get carried away.

Then Jed thought of something else. He felt his face go hot again, and then sighed with secret relief.

He'd never tell anyone how he'd tried to call the police. Now that could have been *really* embarrassing.